Stade de France

Charles de Gaulle t

D0478573

Crêperie

Centre Pompidou

Paris Opéra Garnier

Notre Dame
Île de la Cité

Place de la Bastille

Île St-Louis

Hôtel Quartier Latin

ZOO

Everybo

y Bonjours!

by **Leslie Kimmelman**

illustrated by **Sarah McMenemy**

Alfred A. Knopf ⚞ New York

Monsieur LeMousie says:
In French, *bonjour* (say *bohn-ZHOOR*) means "hello."
Thank you! *Merci!* (say *mehr-SEE*)

When in Paris . . .
everybody bonjours.

From shores.

In stores.

On guided tours.

Everybody bonjours!

Bonjours high.

Bonjours low.

Bonjours fast.

Bonjours slow.
Everybody bonjours!

Every place, it's all bonjouring.
Players scoring.

Batter-pouring.

Height-exploring.

Everybody bonjours!

Bonjours soft.

Bonjours loud.

Bonjour solo.

Bonjour crowd.
Everybody bonjours!

They bonjour

while sweeping floors.

Doing chores.

Eating petits fours.

Bateaux à Louer

Everybody bonjours!

And when our trip is done,

here is how it goes:

When we're home again,

everybody . . .

. . . hellos!

Out and About in Paris

Charles de Gaulle Airport

This airport was named after a famous French general and president. It is the second busiest airport in Europe. A high-speed train carries travelers from the airport to the city.

Le Quartier Latin
Latin Quarter

The Latin Quarter is home to many of Paris's universities, schools, and, of course, students. It is a great neighborhood to explore and is famous for its bookstores, restaurants, theaters, and jazz clubs.

Seine

The beautiful Seine River winds all through Paris—more than thirty bridges cross over it. Even though its name means "new bridge," the Pont Neuf is actually the oldest!

Musée du Louvre
Louvre Museum

The Louvre is one of the world's best-known art museums. Inside the museum is the *Mona Lisa,* the famous painting of a mysterious lady. For hundreds of years, people have argued about whether or not she is smiling. Visitors can enter the Louvre through a glass pyramid that was added to the museum complex in 1989.

Avenue des Champs-Élysées

The Avenue des Champs-Élysées is one of twelve busy avenues that begin at the Arc de Triomphe monument. It is just over a mile long, and is lined on both sides with fancy stores and restaurants.

Tour Eiffel
Eiffel Tower

Built as an attraction for the International Exhibition of 1889, the Eiffel Tower has 1,665 steps and 20,000 lightbulbs, and requires 50 tons of paint. It has been scaled by a mountain climber, was jumped off of by two parachutists, and had a bicycle ridden down its lower portion. Every year, about 6 million people visit the tower.

Le Stade
Stadium

Soccer is the most popular sport in France. In and near Paris it is played at the Stade de France and Parc des Princes stadiums. If you can't get a ticket to a game, try watching one on the giant television screen at the Hôtel de Ville. Yell "*Allez-y!*" with the crowd of fans!

Crêpes

France is world-famous for its cooking. You can find delicious French crêpes (very thin pancakes folded over sweet or savory fillings) at crêpe stands all over Paris. The French also make great breads, chocolates, and cheeses and enjoy eating *escargots*—snails!

Notre Dame

Notre Dame cathedral is a church that took 200 years to build! It is topped with gargoyles—stone monsters that are half man and half beast. The gargoyles are hollow inside and serve as drainpipes—rain runs down from the roof and out the gargoyles' mouths! The French writer Victor Hugo wrote about the cathedral in his famous book *The Hunchback of Notre Dame.*

Zoo

The Jardin des Plantes contains France's oldest zoo. Two of the first animals to live there were a lion and a dog—who eventually shared the same cage! They became friends when, through the bars of the lion's cage, the dog licked a wound on the lion.

centre Pompidou
Pompidou center
A lot of the museums in Paris have art that is very old. The Centre Pompidou was built to give visitors a chance to experience modern art, music, plays, and films. The yellow tubes fastened on the outside of the building are for electrical lines, the green are for water, the red are for heat, and the blue are for ventilation.

opéra Garnier
Garnier Opera
When builders started construction on the site, they were surprised to discover an underground lake! The lake is still under the building's cellar today. Firefighters use it as a water source.

Sacré coeur
Sacré Coeur is a cathedral built on the highest hill in Paris. Because of the color of its stone, many English-speaking visitors refer to it as the white church. Climb up inside the church's dome for an amazing view of the city.

Jardin des Tuileries
Tuileries Gardens
The Tuileries Gardens, built on the grounds of an old roof-tile factory, were designed in the 1600s by King Louis XIV's gardener. In addition to beautiful plants and flowers, the grounds feature an array of statues, a carousel, and a pond for sailing toy boats.

Grande Arche de la Défense
This modern monument looks like a huge open cube. It is located in Paris's business district and has offices inside. In 1999, ten years after it was completed, a climber named Alain Robert scaled the outside of the arch using only his bare hands and feet to get to the top!

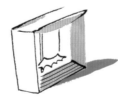

Panthéon
The Panthéon was originally a church and was designed to look like the ancient Roman building of the same name. Many illustrious French citizens are buried here, including authors Victor Hugo and Émile Zola and scientists Marie and Pierre Curie.

For *ma belle* Natalie —L.K.

For coral and Leo —S.M.

THIS IS A BORZOI BOOK PUBLISHED BY ALFRED A. KNOPF

Text copyright © 2008 by Leslie Kimmelman
Illustrations copyright © 2008 by Sarah McMenemy

www.randomhouse.com/kids

Educators and librarians, for a variety of teaching tools, visit us at www.randomhouse.com/teachers

The illustrations in this book were created using mixed media.

Library of Congress Cataloging-in-Publication Data
Kimmelman, Leslie.
Everybody bonjours! / Leslie Kimmelman ; illustrated by Sarah McMenemy. — 1st ed.
p. cm.
SUMMARY: Describes in rhymed text the many ways to use the greeting "Bonjour" when visiting Paris.
ISBN 978-0-375-84443-0 (trade) — ISBN 978-0-375-94443-7 (lib. bdg.)
[1. Salutations—Fiction. 2. Paris (France)—Fiction. 3. France—Fiction. 4. Stories in rhyme—Fiction.] I. McMenemy, Sarah, ill. II. Title.
PZ8.3.K5598Eve 2008
[E]—dc22
2007006899

MANUFACTURED IN CHINA

April 2008

10 9 8 7 6 5 4 3 2 1

First Edition

Grande Arche de la Défense

Sacré Coeur

Arc de Triomphe

Louvre

Le Périphérique

Tour Eiffel

Seine

Boulevard St.-Germain

Café

Pont de Bir-Hakeim

Panthéon